DATE DUE	DATE DUE	DATE DUE	DATE DUE
FEB 26 1986		JUN 16 1992	
APR. 29 1986	AUG 5 1992		
SEP 10 1986	NOV 3 1992		
APR 28 1987			
JUL 13 1987	MAR 2 1994		
AUG. 18 1987			
NOV 28 1987	AUG 19 1994		
APR 4 1988			
JUL 12 1988	AUG 26 1997		
AUG. 16 1988			
OCT 1 1988			
NOV 26 1988			
JUN 12 1990			

RAGGEDY ANN and ANDY'S ANIMAL FRIENDS

Written and Illustrated
by
JOHNNY GRUELLE

THE BOBBS-MERRILL COMPANY, INC.
INDIANAPOLIS • NEW YORK

J

1974

PRINTED IN THE UNITED STATES OF AMERICA

To MARY HESTER HARRISON —

"RABBIT"

THIS BOOK IS AFFECTIONATELY
DEDICATED
♡♡♡
WITH A MAGICAL WISH THAT HER
PATHWAY THROUGH THE GOLDEN
MEADOW OF LIFE MAY BE
BORDERED WITH THE
COSMIC FLOWERS
OF LOVE AND
FRIENDSHIP.

Johnny Gruelle

MIAMI BEACH -
FLORIDA -
MAY 24 - 1935

The Little Brown Bear

THIS is the story about the Little Brown Bear who lived in a hole in a hollow tree.

All winter long the Little Brown Bear slept in his cozy house, curled up in a bed of oak leaves. He slept all night and he slept all day, and he never woke up till winter was over. Then, when the snow was all gone, and the grass was green again, the Little Brown Bear opened his eyes and jumped out of bed and hurried out of his house to look for something for breakfast. He hadn't had anything to eat for months and months and months, and he was a very, very, very hungry Little Brown Bear.

So the Little Brown Bear scrambled down the tree and ran down through the woods as fast as he could go, till he came to a fence, and he climbed the fence and jumped down into a field where there were three cows eating grass; one black cow, one white cow and one red cow.

And the Little Brown Bear said to the black cow:

"Please give me some milk."
And the black cow said: "No."
Then he said to the red cow:
"Please give me some milk."
And the red cow said: "No."
And then he said to the white cow:
"Please give me some milk."

And the white cow said: "Yes, Little Brown Bear."

So the white cow gave him some milk in a little tin pail.

Then the Little Brown Bear said:

"Thank you, nice white cow," and drank up all the milk.

After that he ran on across the field till he came to a fence, and he climbed over that fence and came to a field where there were three pigs eating corn; one black pig, one white pig, and one spotted pig.

And the Little Brown Bear said to the black pig:

"Please give me some corn."

And the black pig said: "No."

Then he said to the white pig:

"Please give me some corn."

And the white pig said: "No."

Then he said to the spotted pig:

"Please give me some corn."

And the spotted pig said: "Yes, Little

Brown Bear." So the spotted pig gave him an ear of yellow corn.

Then the Little Brown Bear said, "Thank you, nice spotted pig," and ate the ear of corn all up.

After that he ran on across the field till he came to a fence, and he climbed over that fence and came to a barnyard where there were three hens sitting on their nests; one black hen, one white hen and one little brown hen.

And the Little Brown Bear said to the black hen:

"Please give me an egg."

And the black hen said: "No."

Then he said to the white hen:

"Please give me an egg."

And the white hen said: "No."

Then he said to the little brown hen:

"Please give me an egg."

And the little brown hen said: "Yes, Little Brown Bear."

So the little brown hen gave him an egg.

Then the Little Brown Bear said:

"Thank you, nice little brown hen," and ate the egg all up.

After that the Little Brown Bear wasn't hungry any more.

Then he walked out of the barnyard and came to a road, and he walked down the road till he came to a place where

there were three ducks swimming on a pond; one black duck, one white duck and one spotted duck with a green head.

And he said to the black duck:

"Please give me a feather."

And the black duck said: "No."

Then he said to the white duck:

"Please give me a feather."

And the white duck said: "No."

Then he said to the spotted duck with a green head:

"Please give me a feather."

And the spotted duck said: "Yes, Little Brown Bear."

So the spotted duck with a green head gave him a feather, and he said, "Thank you, nice spotted duck," and put the feather in his hat for good luck and went on along the road very happy.

After a while the Little Brown Bear climbed a fence and jumped over into a field where there were three horses eating white clover that grew there; one black horse, one gray horse and one white horse.

And the Little Brown Bear said to the black horse:

"Please give me a ride."

And the black horse said: "No."

Then he said to the gray horse:

"Please give me a ride."

And the gray horse said: "No."

Then he said to the white horse:

"Please give me a ride."

And the white horse said: "Yes, Little Brown Bear."

So he climbed up on the fence and jumped on the back of the white horse, and the white horse galloped off across the field till he came to a fence, and he jumped the fence and galloped on down the road.

When the white horse had galloped down the road a great way, the Little Brown Bear saw a leather sack lying in the road, so he said "WHOA!" and jumped off the white horse's back and picked up the leather sack. And when he picked it up it said "Chink!" and

looking inside it the Little Brown Bear saw a great many little, golden pennies.

Then the Little Brown Bear climbed upon the white horse's back again and the white horse galloped down the road until he came to a man driving the black cow, the red cow and the white cow before him. The three cows looked very sad.

“Where are you taking the black cow and the red cow and the white cow?” the Little Brown Bear asked the man.

"I am taking them to market to sell for three golden pennies!" the man said.

So the Little Brown Bear gave the man three golden pennies out of the leather sack and the three cows jumped over the fence and began eating grass; for they were very glad not to go to market.

Then the white horse galloped down the road again until he came to a woman driving the black pig, the white pig and the spotted pig before her.

"Where are you taking the black pig and the white pig and the spotted pig?" the Little Brown Bear asked the woman.

"I am taking them to market to sell for three golden pennies!" the woman said.

So the Little Brown Bear gave the woman three of the golden pennies from the leather sack, and the three pigs climbed over the fence and began eating the corn again, as happy as ever.

And the white horse galloped on down the road again until he came to a boy carrying the black hen and the white hen and the brown hen in a basket.

"Where are you taking the white hen and the black hen and the brown hen?" the Little Brown Bear asked the boy.

"I am taking them to market to sell for three golden pennies!" the boy said.

So the Little Brown Bear gave the boy three golden pennies from the leather sack and the three hens flew over the fence and ran back to their eggs.

And the white horse galloped on down

the road until they came to the pond where the three ducks were swimming, and there they saw a man with a "Bang-gun" ready to shoot the ducks.

"Why do you wish to shoot the black duck and the white duck and the spotted duck with the green head?" the Little Brown Bear asked the man.

"Because I lost my leather sack filled with golden pennies and I can not go to market and buy any food!" the man said.

So the Little Brown Bear gave the man with the "Bang-gun" the leather sack with the golden pennies in it and said: "There are not as many golden pennies in it as there were when I found it, for I bought the black cow and the white cow and the red cow, and the black pig and the white pig and the spotted pig, and the black hen and the white hen and the brown hen!"

Then the man with the "Bang-gun" laughed and said: "Thank you, Little Brown Bear! The leather sack is a very, very magical sack. When anyone takes a golden penny from it another one comes in its place, so you have returned as many golden pennies to me as I lost!"

But when the man with the "Bang-gun" had gone, the three ducks swam up and said, "Thank you, Little Brown Bear, for saving us!"

"You are very welcome!" said the Little Brown Bear.

And the white horse turned around and galloped back up the road for days and days until one day they came to the three hens who cried out: "Thank you, Little Brown Bear, for saving us!" And the Little Brown Bear saw that the black hen had ten little black chickies and the white hen had ten little white chickies and the brown hen had ten little brown chickies, so he said: "You are very welcome!"

And the white horse galloped on up the road until they came to the three pigs.

"Thank you, Little Brown Bear, for saving us!" they said, and the Little Brown Bear saw they had eaten so much corn they were great, big, fat pigs now, so he said: "You are very welcome!"

JOHNNY GRUELLE

And the white horse galloped on up the road until they came to the three cows.

"Thank you for saving us, Little Brown Bear!" they said, and the Little Brown Bear saw that the black cow had a wobbly-legged black calf and the white cow had a wobbly-legged white calf and the red cow had a wobbly-legged red calf, so he said: "You are quite welcome!"

And the white horse galloped on up the road until he came to a fence and

he jumped over the fence and galloped through the woods.

When they came to a big hollow tree the Little Brown Bear said, "WHOA!" and jumped from the white horse's back, for the tree was the same tree in which the Little Brown Bear lived.

"Thank you for the nice ride, white horse!" said the Little Brown Bear as he climbed up to his hole in the tree.

"You are very welcome!" said the white horse as he turned around and galloped away in the darkness, leaving the Little Brown Bear to dream happy dreams all night long, curled up in his bed of oak leaves.

And that's all there is to the story of the Little Brown Bear who lived in a hole in a hollow tree.

Baby Songsparrow

A kindly smile was upon Raggedy Ann's face and her little shoe-button eyes danced with merriment as she turned over in the little toy bed, and raised up on one rag elbow.

Raggedy Andy, who shared Raggedy Ann's bed, slept soundly, his little cotton stuffed head dreaming of pleasant things, and a broad smile stretching across his painted face.

Raggedy Ann shook Raggedy Andy very quietly so as not to disturb the other dolls. "SHH," she whispered as Raggedy Andy raised up. "Let's jump from the window and start on an adventure!"

"All right," Raggedy Andy smiled up at her; so as quietly as two little mice, the two rag dolls tiptoed to the window, and helped each other climb upon the sill.

It was very far to the ground, but Raggedy Ann and Raggedy Andy caught hold of each other's hands and counted, "ONE, TWO, THREE!" and jumped.

Over and over they turned and twisted, the wind catching in Raggedy Ann's dress, and making a balloon.

Near the ground both rag dolls struck a clothes line, and the force of their fall against the rope, sent them spinning back into the air, only to tumble, all doubled up, upon the soft grass.

Raggedy Ann sat up and smoothed out the wrinkles in her apron, and Raggedy Andy sat up too, but one of his rag legs had twisted about in back of his head, and kept him bent forward.

Raggedy Ann hastened to help her friend, and soon the two were racing across the roadway.

"Let's crawl through the hedge," said Raggedy Andy. "There's a lovely magical meadow on the other side, and we may see fairies and every thing."

The two dolls started crawling through a hole in the hedge when Raggedy Ann heard a faint little "Cheepy, Cheepie" close beside her and parting the branches, she saw a tiny little song

I LOVE YOU
JOHNNY GRUELLE.

sparrow with his wings spread out upon the ground, and his tiny baby eyes filled with tears.

Right in front of the little baby song sparrow Raggedy Ann saw a snake.

Raggedy Andy also saw the snake, and with a scramble, he jumped through the leaves, and held the snake's head upon the ground.

My, how the snake wiggled, and twisted and squirmed, and shook. It was all Andy could do to hold it, and even then, the snake sometimes lifted Raggedy Andy clear off the ground.

Raggedy Ann had not been much behind Raggedy Andy.

She picked up the little baby song sparrow as gently as she could and cuddled it against her soft rag body.

"Don't cry," she whispered, "We won't let the snake hurt you. No Sir! Where is your mama?"

At first the little baby song sparrow's heart beat so hard he could not answer, but soon, when Raggedy Ann had smoothed him all over with her cotton stuffed hand, the little baby song sparrow cheeped "My mama went away to get us some breakfast, and I climbed over the edge of the nest and fell to the ground.

My! I was sorry I climbed over the edge of the nest, for I bumped my head on a branch when I fell. Then Gertie Gartersnake came wiggling up to me, and told me to be real still, and she would watch me until my mama came back."

"My goodness," Raggedy Andy laughed from where he was sitting upon Gertie Gartersnake's head. "Didn't the snake intend harming you?"

"No, I didn't!" Gertie Gartersnake said, her voice sounding far away like someone talking with his head under the bed clothes.

At this, Raggedy Andy moved over and said, "Then I'm so sorry, Gertie Gartersnake."

Gertie Gartersnake wiggled her head out from under the leaves where Raggedy Andy had pushed it, and shook the wrinkles out of her bonnet. "You see," Gertie Gartersnake laughed, "I saw the teeny-weeny bird fall out of his nest, and I knew something might find him and hurt him, so I was playing nursemaid until his mama came home."

Soon Mama Songsparrow came fluttering up, and was surprised to see so many visitors. She had a nice beetle, and a fuzzy caterpillar for little Baby Songsparrow, who was always hungry.

Mama Songsparrow pulled the fuzzy caterpillar into three pieces, and offered them to Raggedy Ann, Andy, and Gertie Gartersnake for breakfast. But the three shook their heads, and laughed.

"No, thank you," they said, "Let little teeny Baby Songsparrow have them, so that he will grow strong and fat. Soon we will hear him sing pretty little cheery songs, just like his daddy."

Then Raggedy Ann lifted the teeny weeny song sparrow into his nest, and after shaking hands with Gertie Gartersnake, the two rag dolls said "Good bye," and smiled happily.

They crawled on through the hedge, and, hand in hand, went skipping across the Magic Meadow.

JOHNNY GRUELLE

Eddie Elephant

EDDIE ELEPHANT had only six hairs growing out of his little round-topped head, but Mama Elephant parted them in the middle and placed Eddie's little hat squarely on the part. Then Mama Elephant kissed Eddie Elephant good-bye and stood out on the front porch and watched him run down the path.

Eddie Elephant was very happy as he ran down the path; he had on his nicest new clothes and he was going to spend the day with Gran'ma Elephant and that would be lots of fun.

Eddie Elephant ran down the path until he came to Jungleville.

Yes, there was Uncle Harry Hippopotamus standing in the doorway of his Bakery and when he saw Eddie Elephant coming toward him, Uncle Harry Hippopotamus smiled a great big cheery "Uncley" smile.

"Hello, Eddie Elephant!" laughed Uncle Harry Hippopotamus, "How nice you look."

"Good morning, Uncle Harry Hippopotamus!" said Eddie Elephant, "I have on my nicest new clothes, for I am going to Gran'ma Elephant's house to have a lot of fun and spend the day!"

"I am sure you will have lots of fun, Eddie Elephant!" said Uncle Harry Hippopotamus, as he took Eddie's hand and led him into the Bakery. "I wish you

JOHNNY GRUELLE

would try some of my freshly baked cream puffs, Eddie Elephant; I am not sure whether they are sweet enough!"

Uncle Harry Hippopotamus filled a great sack with cream puffs and patted Eddie Elephant on the back. "You may get hungry on the way to Gran'ma Elephant's!" laughed Uncle Harry Hippopotamus.

Eddie Elephant ate six of the soft fluffy cream puffs and they were very nice. "Thank you, Uncle Harry Hippopotamus!" said Eddie Elephant, "the cream puffs are just sweet enough!"

Uncle Harry Hippopotamus watched Eddie Elephant run down the street of Jungleville until he came to Cousin Katy Kangaroo's lovely Candy Store.

There were many clear glass cases filled with all sorts of nice candies and Eddie Elephant always enjoyed going there, for Cousin Katy Kangaroo let him choose just whatever candies pleased him most.

Cousin Katy Kangaroo saw Eddie Elephant coming down the Jungleville street eating the last of the lovely cream puffs; so she went to the pretty colored marble soda fountain and had an ice cream soda all ready for Eddie Elephant as he walked into her Candy Store.

"Good morning, Eddie Elephant!" said Cousin Katy Kangaroo, "how nice you look!" "I have on my nicest new clothes!" said Eddie Elephant, after he had kissed Cousin Katy Kangaroo "good morning," "I am going over to spend the day with Gran'ma Elephant!"

Cousin Katy Kangaroo put two straws in the glass of soda water, as Eddie Elephant climbed upon the high stools at the counter. "I am not sure that this new flavor is sweet enough!"

"Oh yes, Cousin Katy Kangaroo, the

flavor is just right!" said Eddie Elephant, as he drank all of the soda.

Then Cousin Katy Kangaroo let Eddie Elephant drink six more glasses of soda for, you know, the cream puffs had made him very thirsty. "Thank you very much,

Cousin Katy Kangaroo!" said Eddie Elephant, "I must run along to Gran'ma Elephant's now!"

"I know you will have a nice time!" said Cousin Katy Kangaroo, as she filled a large sack with lovely candy and put a package of chewing gum in Eddie Elephant's pocket.

"Thank you again, Cousin Katy Kangaroo!" Eddie Elephant cried, when he

got to the end of the street and waved his hand to Cousin Katy Kangaroo.

Granny Elephant lived far away from Jungleville and to reach her home Eddie Elephant had to go through the woods and across a great clearing and follow a path through the jungle. The path led right to the center of the jungle and there stood Granny Elephant's house.

When Eddie Elephant came to the great clearing he met a little Cocoa-boy driving a pair of oxen.

The oxen were hitched to a large cart with great round wheels and the cart was loaded heavily with great logs.

When Eddie Elephant came to where the little Cocoa-boy stood he saw that the load was so heavy the great wheels were deep in the mud and the oxen could not pull the cart.

Eddie Elephant said, "Good morning, little Cocoa-boy! Good morning, Oxen!" The little Cocoa-boy and the Oxen said, "Good morning, Eddie Elephant! We are stuck in the mud!"

Then Eddie Elephant gave the little Cocoa-boy and the Oxen each a lovely piece of candy, "When you have eaten that, perhaps you can pull the cart from the mud!" But when the little Cocoa-boy and the Oxen had eaten the lovely candy, they still could not pull the heavy cart from the mud.

"I guess it is too heavy for you!" said Eddie Elephant, as he hung his sack of candy on a bush so the ants would not get in it.

Eddie Elephant took off his pretty little hat and put it on the cart; then he placed his head at the back of the cart and pushed and pushed.

The little Cocoa-boy "Clicked" to the oxen and they pulled and pulled.

And Eddie Elephant pushed and pushed, until presently the cart began to move and the great wheels cried, "Squeekity-squeekity-squeek," and the cart with its heavy load moved out of the mud across the clearing to the good road.

"Thank you very much, Eddie Elephant!" said the little Cocoa-boy.

"You are welcome!" said Eddie Elephant.

"Thank you, Eddie Elephant!" said the two oxen. "You are welcome!" said Eddie Elephant.

"I wish that I had something nice in my pocket to give you for helping us!" said the little Cocoa-boy. Eddie Elephant and the oxen laughed at this, for, you

see, the little Cocoa-boy only had his brown skin for clothes.

"It was fun to help you!" said Eddie Elephant. "I do not expect you to pay me!"

Eddie Elephant gave the little Cocoa-boy and the Oxen a large stick of chew gum apiece. The little Cocoa-boy parted Eddie Elephant's hair, for he had mussed it when he pushed on the cart. And Eddie Elephant left the little Cocoa-boy and the Oxen and the heavy cart, and ran across the clearing to the path through the jungle.

Eddie Elephant walked when he came to the path leading to Granny Elephant's house in the center of the jungle, for there were so many things to see along the path.

Lovely birds with feathers of all colors flew across the path and swung from the great vines hanging from the trees. They called to Eddie Elephant as he passed, and sang pretty songs.

Eddie Elephant stopped whenever he came upon pretty flowers and picked a large bouquet for Granny Elephant.

And where the path led along the river, Eddie Elephant stopped to say "Hello!" to Christopher Crocodile and Alonzo Alligator, for Eddie Elephant always saw them when he went to visit Granny Elephant. Christopher Crocodile and Alonzo Alligator were sitting on a log, smoking their pipes.

"What do you think, Eddie Elephant?" said Christopher Crocodile and Alonzo Alligator. "The strangest thing went up the river a while ago and upon its back were three or four men! What do you think it could be?"

"Did it make a noise like this—'CHUG-CHUG-PUT-PUT?'" asked Eddie Elephant.

"Yes, Eddie Elephant!" said Christopher Crocodile and Alonzo Alligator. "Then it was a boat," said Eddie Elephant. "Sure enough!"

After they had talked and laughed a while, Eddie Elephant left Christopher Crocodile and Alonzo Alligator and walked along the path towards Granny Elephant's house and soon he came to where a great many monkeys lived in the tree tops.

But all the monkeys were away somewhere and Eddie Elephant did not see even old Grandpa Monkey, who usually stayed at home when the others went away.

Eddie Elephant thought this very strange and he said so out loud.

So Eddie Elephant started running along the path, and soon he came to where all the monkeys sat crying.

"Dear me!" said Eddie Elephant. "What is the trouble?"

"They have taken little Mabel Monkey and little Mandy Monkey and little Mickie Monkey and little Maurice Monkey, and carried them away!" all the monkeys cried.

Eddie Elephant knew the monkeys were talking of the men in the boat; so he ran "Klumpity-Klumpity-Klumpity" down the path as fast as he could go, in the direction the men had taken, until he came to where four of the men were eating.

When Eddie Elephant came "Klumpity-Klumpity-Klumpity-Klumpity" right up to them, the men dropped everything and ran to their boat.

Eddie Elephant ran after them and made as much noise as he could, but he could not catch them, for the men jumped into their boat.

Eddie Elephant had to chuckle to himself as he walked back to where the men had been eating their dinner, for they had cut such funny antics when Eddie Elephant surprised them.

But when Eddie Elephant reached the place where the men had been eating their dinners, he saw little Mabel Monkey and little Mandy Monkey and little Mickie Monkey and little Maurice Monkey in a cage, and their little monkey faces were wet with tears. Eddie Elephant knew how he would have felt if someone had carried him away from his dear Mama Elephant; so he unfastened the cage and after wiping all their eyes with his pocket hanky with the little blue border, Eddie Elephant put Mabel Monkey and Mandy Monkey and Mickie Monkey and Maurice Monkey on his back and, telling them to hold tight, he ran "Klumpity-Klumpity-Klumpity" back down the path to where all the monkeys sat crying.

When the monkeys saw Eddie Elephant returning so fast, they thought the men must be after him; so they all scampered into the tree tops.

But when they saw Eddie Elephant with Mabel Monkey and Mandy Monkey and Mickie Monkey and Maurice Monkey on his back, they hurried down and gathered around him.

"Thank you, Eddie Elephant!" said Mabel Monkey's Mama.

"You are welcome!" said Eddie Elephant.

"Thank you, Eddie Elephant!" said Mandy Monkey's Mama.

"You are welcome!" said Eddie Elephant.

"Thank you, Eddie Elephant!" said Mickie Monkey's Mama.

"You are welcome!" said Eddie Elephant.

"Thank you, Eddie Elephant!" said Maurice Monkey's Mama.

"You are welcome!" said Eddie Elephant.

Then all the Monkeys said, "Thank you, Eddie Elephant!" and Eddie Elephant said, "You are welcome!"

And all were very happy again.

Then when Eddie Elephant said good-bye to all the monkeys, Grandpa Monkey whispered to the other monkeys and they nodded their heads.

Then Grandpa Monkey said to Eddie Elephant, "We wish to give you something for helping us!"

"I do not expect you to do that!" said Eddie Elephant, "I helped you because one should always help those who are in trouble and I am very glad that I could make you all happy."

"Yes, yes, we know how kind you are, Eddie Elephant!" said Grandpa Monkey. "But just the same, we wish to give you something; so I will show you the way, if you will take me upon your back, to a place known only to the monkeys, and you must promise never to show the place to anyone else!"

"Then I promise!" said Eddie Elephant, as he took Grandpa Monkey upon his back.

Grandpa Monkey pointed the way to Eddie Elephant and soon they came to a field. Eddie Elephant stopped in surprise when he saw the field, for he had never known there was a field there. Everywhere were colored flowers. Red and white

and green and yellow and pink and black flowers growing upon slender stalks.

But when Eddie Elephant walked close to the flowers, he knew in a second that they were not flowers. They were lollypops growing wild.

The red lollypops were strawberry flavor, the white ones were vanilla flavor, the green ones were lime flavor, the yellow ones were lemon flavor, the pink ones were cherry flavor, and the black ones were licorice flavor.

Now if there was anything that Eddie Elephant liked, it was lollypops; so when Grandpa Monkey told Eddie Elephant to help himself, Eddie Elephant filled all his pockets with the pretty lollypops. And Grandpa Monkey filled his pockets with lollypops, too, for he wanted to take them back to Mabel and Mandy and Mickie and Maurice Monkey.

Then Grandpa Monkey went over to one side of the field and showed Eddie Elephant a barn.

"Stay here and shut your eyes tightly and do not open them until I tell you!" said Grandpa Monkey.

Eddie Elephant could hardly keep from peeping just a little bit, but he didn't.

Soon Grandpa Monkey said, "Open your eyes!"

You probably would never guess what the surprise was that Grandpa Monkey had for Eddie Elephant; so I must tell you.

When Eddie Elephant opened his eyes he saw the loveliest blue, shiny bicycle with rubber tires and nickel-plated wheels and a little bell which went, "TINKLE-TINKLE," when it was touched.

Eddie Elephant thanked Grandpa Monkey over and over again and he carried the pretty blue bicycle to the path and with Grandpa Monkey upon his back, Eddie Elephant rode the bicycle back to where the Monkeys all sat waiting.

Eddie Elephant was very, very happy, and he gave every monkey a lollypop and did not mind in the least when he had none left for himself.

Then Eddie Elephant thanked the Monkeys all again and rode his pretty blue, shiny bicycle down the path towards Granny Elephant's house.

The farther Eddie Elephant rode his pretty blue, shiny bicycle down the path, the faster he could make it go, and he tinkled his bell at every bend so that he would not bump into anyone who might be coming along.

And so Eddie Elephant went skimming along until he came to where Bertram Buffalo lived. Bertram Buffalo lived with his Mama all alone in the jungle, and did not have a nice Grandma to go spend the day with, as did Eddie Elephant. Nor did Bertram Buffalo have a nice Uncle Harry Hippopotamus who owned a Bakery filled with cookies and pies and fluffy cream puffs. Nor did Bertram Buffalo have a nice Cousin Katy Kangaroo who owned a lovely Candy Store with clear glass counters filled with candy and a lovely marble soda fountain. Bertram Buffalo had only three cocoa-nuts to play with and had never even tasted ice cream; so you may know how poor Bertram Buffalo's Mama must have been.

"Hello, Eddie!" said Bertram Buffalo.

"Hello, Bertram!" said Eddie Elephant.

"You have a very pretty blue, shiny bicycle with nickel-plated handle-bars and a bell which goes, 'TINKLE-TINKLE!'" said Bertram.

Eddie Elephant jumped from his nice blue, shiny bicycle and said, "You may ride it, Bertram Buffalo!" And he helped Bertram Buffalo upon the pretty blue, shiny bicycle and showed him how to make it go.

Bertram Buffalo rode the bicycle awhile and Eddie Elephant rode it awhile, and they had lots of fun taking turns.

Eddie Elephant knew he should be getting along towards Grandma Elephant's home, for he still had a long way to go, but Bertram Buffalo liked to ride the pretty blue bicycle so well, Eddie Elephant did not like to take it away.

"I tell you what, Bertram Buffalo," said Eddie Elephant, "I would like to give you the pretty blue, shiny bicycle with the rubber tires, the nickel-plated handle-bars and the little bell which says, 'TINKLE-TINKLE!'"

Bertram Buffalo's eyes sparkled with happiness, but then he said, "It is a very, very pretty, blue, shiny bicycle, Eddie Elephant, and I would love to have it to play with, but if you give it to me, you would not have it to enjoy yourself!"

"It is yours, Bertram Buffalo!" said Eddie Elephant, "Take it in and show it to your Mama!"

So Bertram Buffalo rode the pretty blue, shiny bicycle with the rubber tires and the nickel-plated handle-bars and the little bell which said, "TINKLE-TINKLE," around the side of his house to where Mama Buffalo was doing the neighbor's washing. And as soon as Bertram Buffalo turned the corner of his house, Eddie Elephant ran down the path until he came to the center of the jungle and Granny Elephant's home.

Granny Elephant heard Eddie Elephant singing long before he came in sight and she ran out to the front gate to meet him.

Eddie Elephant put his arms around Granny Elephant and told her all about his adventures.

Granny Elephant kissed him and said, "You are a nice kindly little elephant, Eddie Elephant, and I am so glad you came to see Granny and that you helped your friends who were in trouble. Even if kindly Grandpa Monkey had given you nothing, you would have had the pleasure of knowing you had given the Mama monkeys happiness. And after all, you did the kindest thing when you gave what you liked best of all to little Bertram Buffalo!"

"I know it was nice, Granny," said Eddie Elephant, "for while I wanted the pretty, blue, shiny bicycle with the rubber tires and the nickel-plated handle-bars and the little bell which said 'TINKLE-TINKLE,' when you touched it, still when I gave it to Bertram Buffalo, I felt all tingly with happiness inside!"

Then Granny Elephant led Eddie Elephant into the dining room where she had just prepared dinner, and as Eddie Elephant had had a long happy journey that morning he was very, very hungry. Eddie Elephant ate twenty palm leaf pies, fifty-seven jelly tarts, ninety-six fluffy doughnuts, twenty boiled ostrich eggs and a lot of bread and butter.

While eating, he fell asleep, sitting in the chair. Granny Elephant carried little Eddie Elephant to the couch and made him quite comfortable, and then she went about her work, singing softly to herself so as not to disturb the pleasant dreams that floated through the little round head of kindly little Eddie Elephant.

The Gnome and the Woodpeckers

At one spot in the Golden Meadow, Raggedy Ann and Raggedy Andy came to where a log lay across the looking-glass brook, and there beside the log, almost hidden in the tall grasses, the Raggedys found a little, itty-bitty candy-covered cookie bush.

When Raggedy Andy picked some of the tiny candy-covered cookies for Raggedy Ann and handed them to her, the teensy-weensy candy covered cookies grew larger.

"I guess they are magical candy-covered cookies," Raggedy Andy said as he picked some for himself and sat beside Raggedy Ann on the log.

"Let's let our feet down in the water and make ripples," Raggedy Ann suggested. "Then we can pretend the looking-glass brook is smiling at us."

"Yes. Let's do," Raggedy Andy agreed. "And, Raggedy Ann, maybe the ripples on a brook is really the brook's way of smiling."

"It must be, Raggedy Andy," Raggedy Ann laughed as she splashed her rag feet around in the water. "Isn't the water in the smiling brook nice and cool?"

"Yes," Raggedy Andy replied. "It makes my feet feel so cool and soggy."

"You had better not sit with your feet in the water too long," a little old Gnome said, as he came out upon the log and sat down beside Raggedy Andy. "You may catch the Eppizoodiz in your toes."

"Don't you believe it," Raggedy Ann said, even though she knew the Gnome was joking, for she saw him put his feet in the water as soon as he sat down. "We are made of cloth and stuffed with nice, clean white cotton, and even when we jump in the looking-glass brook we do not get the Eppizoodiz anywhere in our rag bodies."

"I am glad of that," the little old Gnome said. "I have just come from Winnie Woodpecker's home in the old, old, dead tree, the one way over there holding up its arms toward the popcorn clouds, and all three of the little baby Woodpeckers have caught cold from sitting with their heads out of the window when it was raining."

"Dear me!" Raggedy Ann said.

"Would you believe it?" the little old Gnome asked. "All three of the woodpecker babies have such colds it has made their heads red."

Raggedy Andy wiggled one shoe-button eye at Raggedy Ann. "Mister Gnome," Raggedy Andy asked, "do you know what the three baby woodpeckers are named?"

"Oh, yes," the little old Gnome replied, "One of the babies is named Wallie after his uncle Wallace Woodpecker, one Willie, and the other Woolie."

Raggedy Andy again wiggled his shoe-button eye at Raggedy Ann.

"Why do you wiggle your shoe-button eye at Raggedy Ann?" the little old Gnome asked.

"Because," Raggedy Andy replied, "that is the only way I can wink."

"But why should you wink, Raggedy Andy?" the little old Gnome wished to know.

"Because, I do not believe you know much about woodpeckers," Raggedy Andy said as he

JOHNNY GRUELLE

gave the little old Gnome another candy-covered cookie. "For, if you did, you would know the little woodpeckers have red heads, not because they have caught cold, but because they are all boy Woodpeckers. If any of the baby Woodpeckers had not had red heads, it would have been because they were girl Woodpeckers. All boy Woodpeckers have red heads and all girl Woodpeckers have black heads."

"Well, I'm glad of that," the little old Gnome chuckled, "because the Woodpeckers are really very nice creatures. If it wasn't for their work upon the trees, the bugs would soon kill all of the trees. Then we would miss the lovely leaves and the cool shade. But," he went on, "I just supposed the Woodpeckers had colds and that it made their heads red like colds make noses red."

And the little old Gnome chuckled so hard, he got Raggedy Ann and Raggedy Andy chuckling so hard, the log began jiggling and all three, Raggedy Ann, the little old Gnome and Raggedy Andy tumbled off the log, backwards into the water where they splashed around and had so much fun they sent smiles way up the face of the looking-glass brook beyond where it made a bend at the pussy willow bushes.